To my son, Oakland Jack - I can't wait to meet you!
- Mr. Jay

For Noah and Risako, sharing adventures everyday
- Gary

New Paige Press, LLC
NewPaigePress.com

New Paige Press and the distinctive ladybug icon are registered trademarks of New Paige Press, LLC

Text copyright © 2020 by New Paige Press
Illustrations copyright © 2020 by Gary Wilkinson

ISBN 978-0-578-55758-8

Printed and bound in China

New Paige Press provides special discounts when purchased in larger volumes for premiums and promotional purposes, as well as for fundraising and educational use. Custom editions can also be created for special purposes. In addition, supplemental teaching material can be provided upon request. For more information, please visit NewPaigePress.com

NEW PAIGE PRESS

New Paige Press is an imprint of
LYRIC & STONE
PUBLISHING

PATRICK PICKLEBOTTOM
AND THE PENNY BOOK

Story by
Mr. Jay

Artwork by
Gary Wilkinson

Young Patrick Picklebottom,
who was always so poor,
had only a penny
when he entered the store.

He walked past the candy, some toys and a ball,
to the one thing he wished he could buy most of all.

Unable to purchase,
and resigned to just look,
he longingly gazed
at a dusty old book.

"Would you like to buy this?"
asked an elderly man.
"I'd like to," said Patrick,
"but I don't think I can.

I've only one penny,
and not one penny more,"
then he hung his head low
and turned toward the door.
"As it happens," replied
the kind-hearted gent,
"this book only costs
a single red cent."

"Thank you so much!"
Patrick said to the man.
Then, clutching his book,
he turned 'round and ran,
anxious for home,
to bask in the glory,
of his amazing new book,
and its incredible story.

He had made it three blocks, when he saw his friend Tom,
on the steps of his porch, staring down at his palm.
In his hands was a smartphone, and he was swiping away,
but stopped for a moment, to look up and say,
"Hey, Patrick! Come here, I've got this new app -
it shows me new pictures each time that I tap."

"Pictures of what?
And why would I care?"
But Tom just looked up
with a frustrated glare.
"They're shots from all over,
there's always a bunch...
Here look, some girl posted
a pic of her lunch!

How else will you know
what the world is about?"
Patrick looked at his book,
"I guess I'll find out."

He continued towards home,
through a park, 'round a tree,
when he heard a voice call,
"Hey, Patrick! Come see!"
And he saw his friend Donna
staring up at the sky,
but it took him a moment
to understand why.

Up in the air,
in the clouds, all alone,
floating above them
was a stealthy white drone.
It veered to the left,
then swung toward the sun,
as Donna exclaimed,
"See? Isn't this fun?"

Looking confused,
Patrick wondered aloud,
"I guess it'd be neat
to be up in a cloud.
But you're on the ground,
and you're standing real still,
so I'm sorry, but I guess
I just don't see the thrill."

Donna looked stunned,
then she said with a sigh,
"The thrill is controlling
machines that can fly.
How else can we capture
the excitement of flight?"
Patrick looked at his book,
and he clutched it real tight.

Leaving the park, and back on the run,
he was close to his home, as the sky lost the sun.
He was at his front door, with his hand on the knob,
when he suddenly heard his neighbor-friend, Bob.

" Patrick, you're home! Come have a look,
I've a new video game, so put down that old book!"

" It's called 'Monsters Clash!' for my GameStation Five,
and I've waited two weeks for this game to arrive.
We capture these beasts who've escaped from their collars..."
"But that game," Pat exclaimed, "costs three hundred dollars!"
Bob just replied, "How else can you battle monsters all day?"
But Pat clutched his book and said, "I might have a way."

Up in his room, tucked into his bed,
with a single small lamp aglow near his head,
he read through his book, every page without fail,
each chapter a story, its own separate tale.

He read about kingdoms, and lands far and wide,
where heroes and monsters and dragons collide.
He read about rockets blasting out past the moon,
and as his eyes closed, he knew that real soon
he'd dream of adventures, and of course there'd be many,
from a book that he'd bought... for a single red penny.